Weekly Reader Presents

Gobo and the Prize from Outer Space

By Lyn Calder • Pictures by Frederic Marvin

Muppet Press
Henry Holt and Company
NEW YORK

Published by Henry Holt and Company,
521 Fifth Avenue, New York, New York 10175.

Library of Congress Cataloging in Publication Data
Calder, Lyn.
Gobo and the prize from outer space.
Summary: Arguing over who gets to use the bicycle
they hope to win in a contest, five friends in Fraggle
Rock have a terrible fight and stop speaking to each
other.
[1. Contests—Fiction.   2. Friendship—Fiction.
3. Bicycles and bicycling—Fiction.   4. Puppets—
Fiction]   I. Marvin, Frederic, ill.   II. Title.
PZ7.C136Go   1986   [E]   85-17598
ISBN: 0-03-007243-3

Printed in the United States of America

ISBN 0-03-007243-3

HERE'S *my chance*, thought Gobo Fraggle, peeking into Doc's workshop. *The Hairy Beast is asleep.*

Gobo stared at Doc's wastebasket, where he hoped to find a postcard from his Uncle Traveling Matt. He loved reading about his uncle's adventures with the Silly Creatures in Outer Space.

Gobo took a deep breath and dashed inside.

"Woof, woof!" barked the beast, leaping up.

Gobo froze in his tracks. Would he be able to reach the basket? Or would the Hairy Beast get him this time?

Brave adventurer that he was, Gobo raced to the basket, grabbed the card, and ran.

Gobo didn't stop running until he was halfway back to the Great Hall. He was still out of breath when he found his best friends—Wembley, Boober, Mokey, and Red—by the pool.

"I have a card from my Uncle Matt," panted Gobo, waving it proudly. "And did I have a hard time getting this one!"

Gobo began to read the card to his friends.

" 'Dear Resident: You have been chosen by Captain Corn's Prize Headquarters to enter our GIANT SWEEP-STAKES—' "

"Uh, Gobo, I hate to interrupt," said Mokey, "but I don't believe anyone here is named Resident."

Gobo looked at the card and groaned. "I must have grabbed the wrong one."

"Why don't you read it anyway," said Red. "It sounds much more interesting than anything your Uncle Matt ever has to say."

Gobo gave Red a grumpy look, but he continued reading. " 'To win one of the great prizes shown on this card, just write your favorite numbers in the boxes below. Put the gold star next to the prize of your choice. Then fill in your name and return the card TODAY!' "

"Wow!" Gobo said. "We just fill in some numbers, and we win a prize. It must be some kind of Outer Space magic!"

"Now you're talking," said Red. "I love magic, and I *love* prizes. Let's see, there are five of us. So put number five in a box for me."

Gobo wrote the number five in the first box.

"I'll pick five, too," said Wembley.

"You can't pick two numbers," said Gobo. "Just pick one."

"Okay, one," said Wembley, shrugging his shoulders.

Mokey seemed to be in a trance. "Eight," she said finally. "I like the continuous motion of the line."

"Seven is my lucky number," said Gobo, putting a seven in one of the boxes. "How about you, Boober? What number do you want?"

"Four," Boober replied. "I have four baskets of laundry to do. Can we get on with this?"

Gobo read the list of prizes. "The first prize is one million dollars."

"That sure is a lot of dollars," said Wembley. "What are dollars?"

"They look like leaves," Boober muttered. "*Poison* leaves."

"Here's the next prize," said Gobo. "An all-expense-paid trip to New York City."

"That's a tasty-looking Doozer construction," said Mokey, "but we already have enough to eat."

"Look at this prize!" said Gobo. "A ten-speed Huzza-Huzza bicycle. My Uncle Matt wrote to me about bicycles. You can ride around really fast and carry lots of things in the basket."

"Sounds like fun!" said Red. "Let's put our star there."

They all agreed. Then, with Wembley at his side in case of trouble, Gobo returned the card to Doc's workshop.

When Gobo and Wembley got back, they found their friends talking about how they would use the prize if they won.

"I'll ride it to the Gorgs' Garden to collect radishes," Mokey said.

"Just think how much laundry I'll be able to carry," sighed Boober. "Of course I'll probably fall off and break both my legs."

"And think how far I can go exploring," said Gobo.

"I'll go with you!" Wembley said.

"Hold everything!" shouted Red. "By the time I get to ride the thing, it will be all worn out! I'm riding first!"

That started the fight.

"No, you're not!" Gobo yelled. "Who risked his life getting the card? I'm riding first!"

"Who risks her life every day in the Gorgs' Garden?" asked Mokey. "I'm the one who really needs the prize."

"What about your laundry?" Boober said angrily.

"Well . . . well," Wembley spluttered, "what about me?"

The shouting went on for an hour. It finally ended in angry silence. The Fraggle friends were determined never to speak to each other again.

To calm down, Mokey tried writing a poem . . . while Red cooled off with a triple-twist dive.

Boober decided never to cook anything for his ex-friends again. So he made the tiniest radish pie in the history of Fraggle Rock.

Wembley didn't know what to do. He tried throwing a temper tantrum. He tried sulking. He even tried acting as though he didn't care.

As the days went by, Gobo did some serious thinking. It wasn't like Fraggles to stay angry so long. After all, they were good friends. *And good friends work things out*, Gobo decided.

Then he got an idea. It wasn't easy, but he convinced his four friends to come to a meeting at the Great Hall.

"I've got the solution!" he told them. "If we win the bicycle, we'll pick Doozer sticks to see who rides first. The one who gets the longest stick wins."

"How about the shortest stick?" said Red, still being difficult.

"Now, let's be sensible," said Mokey. "If we keep fighting this way, no one will get to ride the bicycle."

Boober and Wembley agreed.

"Okay, okay," said Red. "Let's go and see if we won."

Gobo slipped into Doc's workshop while the others waited in the tunnel. He was back in an instant, laughing so hard that his sides hurt.

"What are you laughing about?" asked Boober.

Gobo pointed to Outer Space.

Inside the workshop was their prize—a shiny new yellow bicycle. But it looked big enough for a Gorg! It would never fit through the hole in the wall. Gobo's friends burst out laughing. All their fighting had been for nothing.

"Who needs a bicycle anyway?" said Wembley.

"That's right," said Red. "In fact I say we have a who-needs-a-bicycle party! Last one in the pool is a soggy radish!"

While the others raced back, Gobo stayed behind. He was listening to an argument in Doc's workshop.

"My good friend," a deep voice boomed. "I know you want to visit the spaniel down the road, but you can't ride the bicycle first. I need it to get my new rain-making machine over to the weather station."

Gobo turned away. *They're sure acting like silly creatures,* he thought. *But if they really are good friends, they'll work it out. Good friends always do.*